Kate, the ghost dog

Coping With the Death of a Pet

by Wayne L. Wilson
illustrated by Soud

Magination Press Washington, DC
American Psychological Association

In memory of Kate — WLW
To my brother, Rudy — RS

Published by
MAGINATION PRESS
An Educational Publishing Foundation Book
American Psychological Association
750 First Street, NE
Washington, DC 20002

For more information about our books, including a complete catalog, please write
to us, call 1-800-374-2721, or visit our website at www.maginationpress.com.

Printed by Worzalla, Stevens Point, Wisconsin

Library of Congress Cataloging-in-Publication Data

Wilson, Wayne L.
Kate, the ghost dog : coping with the death of a pet /
by Wayne L. Wilson ; illustrated by Soud.
p. cm.
Summary: With the help of her family and friends,
Aleta tries to cope with the death of her beloved dog, Kate.
ISBN-13: 978-1-4338-0554-7 (hardcover : alk. paper)
ISBN-10: 1-4338-0554-5 (hardcover : alk. paper)
ISBN-13: 978-1-4338-0555-4 (pbk. : alk. paper)
ISBN-10: 1-4338-0555-3 (pbk. : alk. paper) [1. Grief--Fiction. 2. Death--Fiction.
3. Dogs--Fiction. 4. Friendship--Fiction. 5. Family life--Fiction.] I. Soud, ill. II. Title.

PZ7.W6993Kat 2010
[Fic]--dc22
2009019045

10 9 8 7 6 5 4 3 2 1

First Printing September 2009

Contents

A Girl's Best Friends

Friday afternoon, as soon as school let out, Aleta and her best friends, Cassie and Nina, raced on rollerblades to her house. As usual, Cassie won. She was one of the best athletes in the school. Tapping her foot impatiently, Cassie waited until they caught up to her at Aleta's front gate before crowing: "LADIES AND GENTLEMEN, THE ROLLERBLADE CHAMPION OF THE WORLD: CASSIEEEEE MOORE!"

She triumphantly raised her hands in the air and hopped up and down, cupping her hands around her mouth to mimic a crowd roar. Then she broke into her signature silly dance. Aleta and Nina ignored her at first, but before long they tackled her and they all tumbled to the ground, laughing giddily. Not only was Cassie's laugh contagious, just watching her was hilarious. Cassie was a redhead with a face sprinkled with freckles that seemed to move whenever she talked. And when she laughed, her face scrunched up, tears flew, and she hugged her stomach like she was in pain. Pretty soon all three girls were holding their stomachs from laughing so hard.

After a while, Aleta asked, "How come Kate's not barking? She hates the sound of rollerblades."

"Yeah, I was wondering the same thing," Cassie said, wiping her tears away.

"Oh, she's probably asleep in the house," Nina replied. "Hey, you guys want to get some ice cream?"

"Ooooooh, that sounds really good," Aleta said, rubbing her hands.

Cassie's eyes widened. "Yeah, I want the chocolate peanut butter crunch!"

"I want the mint yogurt," Nina said, closing her eyes and licking her lips.

"Well let's go!" Cassie shouted, spinning on her skates.

"Wait, Cassie! I have to take Kate on a walk first," Aleta said, opening the gate.

Cassie grabbed the fence to stop herself. "Let's take her with us! She likes ice cream, too."

"Loves it," Aleta chuckled. "Come on. Let's get her. But you guys have to take off your skates before you come inside the house."

"Okay. When we come back, can we play fashion show?" Nina asked as she sat on the ground and unstrapped her rollerblades. Nina was really pretty with wavy brown hair. She planned on being a super model when she grew up, that or a fashionista.

Kate was a real diva.

"Again?" Cassie groaned.

"Oh, come on, Cass. You know it's fun. We can dress Kate up again and put sunglasses on her. Then we'll make a runway for her to walk down after a hair makeover."

"You mean a fur makeover," Cassie laughed.

"Whatever...it will be fun. You can be our fashion photographer for the model shoot."

"I don't want to be that kind of photographer. And besides, I'm not going to be a photographer until I win my Olympic gold medals in track."

"You can still practice. And since Aleta's going to be a

veterinarian, she can be our in-house doctor and make sure our model is healthy and eating right."

"I don't know...Kate's a real diva," Aleta joked.

Cassie raised her eyebrows. "Uh, oh, she might mistake me for paparazzi and try to bite me!"

"That's okay. We have a doctor in the house for emergencies."

"Uh, uh...I'm a vet. I only work on animals, not humans."

"That's harsh! Then I guess you'll have to run, Cassie. At least you'll be in shape for the Olympics," Nina laughed.

Cassie clapped her hands. "Great! I love it when she chases me!"

They passed Aleta's mom and dad watching TV and reading the paper in the living room.

"Hey, girls," Aleta's mom said.

"Hi!" the girls yelled back.

"What are you up to, Aleta?"

"We're taking Kate with us to get some ice cream!"

The sound on the TV lowered and Aleta's dad peered over his newspaper. "Fine, just don't give her any ice cream. It's not good for dogs. The last time you did that I had to clean up after her. And that was no party."

The girls cringed as they looked at each other. Cassie pinched her nose and suppressed a giggle.

"Okay, Daddy. Um, do you know where Kate is?" Aleta asked, jingling her leash.

"Last I checked, she was sleeping in your bedroom," he said and went back to his paper.

Chapter 2

The Worst Day Ever

Aleta whistled loudly and jingled the leash again as they walked down the hall to her bedroom. *That's weird*, Aleta thought. Usually once Kate heard the leash she was jumping at her heels, barking, growling, and playfully grabbing it with her mouth. Aleta hoped her little brother, Darnell, hadn't accidentally left the gate open again. The last time he did that she was furious with him. Luckily, their neighbors spotted Kate wandering down the sidewalk and brought her home.

Aleta was relieved to find Kate lying at the foot of her bed.

"There you are. Get up, girl! Time for a walk."

But she didn't move. Suddenly, Aleta's stomach felt queasy.

"What's wrong with her?" Cassie asked in a hushed voice.

"There's nothing wrong with her, Cassie," Aleta said.

"Kate, come on...wake up...walkeeeee...walkeeeee!" she said frantically.

Nothing.

Nina leaned over Kate. "She's not moving. I think she's d—"

"Shut up, Nina! You don't know what you're talking about. Move out the way!" snapped Aleta.

Aleta didn't really mean to snap at Nina. It just kind of slipped out. Nina stepped back and clung to Cassie's arm. Tears ran down Cassie's cheeks. This time it wasn't from laughter.

Aleta's face tightened. *Cassie and Nina are being so stupid!*

"KATE!" Aleta yelled, stomping her feet to get Kate's attention.

Kate didn't wiggle or even twitch like she ordinarily did when she was sleeping. Her chest wasn't rising or falling either. Aleta could feel herself getting more anxious.

"Kate, please get up," Aleta pleaded softly. Trembling, she bent down and gently shook Kate's body. Aleta was so shocked to feel how stiff it was that she fell backwards. "Mommy! Daddy!" Aleta screamed. "Something's wrong with Kate!"

Her parents raced into the bedroom.

"What is it, honey?" Aleta's dad asked, panicked.

They kneeled down beside Aleta, and her mom said, "Oh no...poor Kate...looks like she's been here awhile. Oh honey, I'm so sorry..."

Aleta didn't want to hear that. Kate was fine when she left for school that morning. How did this happen? It didn't make sense.

Aleta couldn't give up on her. "Kate, please don't die... please..."

Aleta's mom turned to her, eyes tearing, "Baby, I'm sorry... she's gone."

"No she's not! We need to take her to a vet. She'll be okay. You'll see."

She tugged on her dad's arm. "Why are we wasting time? We need to take her to a doctor. NOW!" she sobbed.

No one said a word. They just stared at her. Aleta didn't understand. *How can they just stand there and do nothing? Don't they realize that Kate's not dead? She's sleeping and alive! Why doesn't anyone believe me? Don't they want to save Kate?*

Her dad caressed her shoulder. "It's too late, Aleta."

"No it's not! She's still alive! You guys are lying to me! She's not dead!"

Aleta pushed his hand away and wrapped her arms around Kate. She kissed and hugged her so tightly her dad had to gently pull Aleta's arms from around her furry neck. She didn't want to let go. She couldn't.

Aleta cried so hard she buried her head into her dad's chest and fell into his big strong arms.

Chapter 3
Leave Me Alone!

It was quiet in her room, but Aleta couldn't fall asleep. She just cried and cried and thought about Kate. *Kate wasn't that old. Why did she have to die? Why did she leave me?*

Sometime during the night, the door slowly creaked open. "Aleta, are you awake?"

It was her mom.

Aleta pretended to be asleep. Her mom stood briefly at the door and then tiptoed over to the bed. She crawled under the covers and snuggled her daughter in her arms. Aleta didn't resist. It felt good to be held and comforted by her mom. Eventually, she fell asleep.

The next morning Aleta woke up to the sound of digging in the back yard. She rose from her bed, groggy and wanting to go back to sleep. Aleta's stomach gurgled, probably because she didn't eat dinner last night. She had no appetite. She wanted to go straight to bed. She wanted to be left alone. Later in the evening her brother knocked and asked if he could come in. She answered by throwing a shoe at the door.

Aleta wished she could go back to sleep again. The digging noises were irritating. Occasionally the shovel clinked against hard earth, but the digging continued. She knew why. Last night her dad held a family meeting at the kitchen table before she went to bed. Her mom made hot cocoa. Aleta's dad felt Kate should be given a proper burial. He said that they were lucky to live in a town where you could bury your pet in your own back yard. "Some cities don't allow this," he said. He asked if they should bury Kate at home or somewhere else, or if they should have Kate cremated.

Darnell was so upset by this he almost spilled his cocoa. "No! I don't want her to burn up! I don't want her to feel any pain."

His mom kissed him on the cheek and embraced him. "Oh, no, honey, Kate is dead. She won't feel any pain. I promise."

"I still don't want that!"

"How about if we bury Kate in a pet cemetery?" their dad asked.

"You mean a cemetery only for dogs?"

"Dogs and all kinds of animals."

Darnell smiled through his tears. "That's kind of cool... she might like that. You think so, Lee?" He always called her

Lee because he couldn't pronounce her name when he was younger.

Aleta looked at Darnell, and it shocked her when these words flew out of her mouth:

"No. Bury her here! This is her home. This is where she belongs."

No one disagreed.

"You kids want to be there for the burial?"

"No," Aleta quickly said.

"Me, neither," echoed Darnell. He reached for Aleta's hand but she moved it away.

"We understand," their mom said, "But if you kids change your minds, we'd love you to join us."

Aleta didn't hear the rest. She was already headed to her bedroom.

It seemed like the digging went on forever. Aleta clapped her hands to her ears. The sound was annoying. Still, Aleta got curious and parted the curtains. Peeking out the window, she saw her dad shoveling a deep hole in the corner of the backyard. He was hard at work and drenched in sweat. Aleta saw that he took his job seriously as he stopped to rest, but only for a moment. She felt proud he was doing all of this for Kate and their family. Soon Aleta's mom and little brother walked into the yard

to join him. *What's Darnell doing there? He said he didn't want to be there.* Darnell looked scared and clung to his mom's arm. Unexpectedly, her mom turned and looked at Aleta's window. She gestured for Aleta to come join them. Aleta shook her head, no. Her mom seemed okay with that. She offered her daughter a warm smile.

Aleta's dad laid the shovel on the ground and surveyed the hole. That's when she spied the thick bundle of blankets nearby. He bent down and picked them up. Her dad cradled the blankets in his arms and held them for a moment, slowly shaking his head. Then he gently lowered the bundle into the ground. Aleta's mom held Darnell's hand and affectionately put her arm around her dad's waist as they stared into the hole. A few words were spoken and her dad reached for the shovel again. She couldn't watch any longer.

Aleta felt so heavy and her throat felt like she had swallowed a bunch of cotton balls. She almost ripped the curtains jerking them together.

Then it hit Aleta. Kate was wrapped inside those blankets, the same ones she slept on every night in her dog bed. Aleta hoped for a miracle that somehow Kate would wake up from her deep sleep, wrestle her way out of those blankets, and leap from her grave.

Chapter 4

A Sad Memorial

Later in the day, Aleta's mom came to her room and announced that she and her dad wanted to have a memorial service for Kate. Aleta protested immediately.

"Do I have to go?"

"Yes."

"Can't I just watch from my window?" she begged.

"Not this time," her mom firmly stated. "This is something we need to do as a family. It would be good for us to pay our respects to Kate and say our final goodbyes."

"I don't want to."

"Aleta, I know it's difficult, but a memorial service is something positive. We're going to celebrate Kate's life, not mourn it."

Aleta crossed her arms, pouting.

"Cassie and Nina are going to be there."

"I don't care."

"You're going."

And that ended their discussion.

When Aleta finally went outside with her family for the memorial, she saw Cassie and Nina, along with her dad's uncle, James Davis. Everyone called him Uncle Jimmy, even Cassie and Nina. He had been the caretaker and gardener at Rose Park, a few blocks away, since Aleta's parents were kids. Aleta had never met Mrs. Davis. She died before Aleta was born. And they never had any children. But they made up for it with all the dogs and cats that lived with them and still lived with Uncle Jimmy. Plus they loved to spend their time gardening.

Kate was the most intelligent dog I have ever known...

Everyone looked happy to see her. But all Aleta really noticed was the orange-red sunset that reminded her of Kate's golden fur.

Earlier in the day, Aleta's dad asked if she wanted to put some of Kate's stuff in the grave before he covered it. "No," she replied. She wanted to keep her leash, collar, dog bowl, and anything that reminded her of Kate.

During the memorial, Aleta's dad asked each of them to take a handful of dirt he had shoveled to the side and throw it into the grave to symbolically say goodbye to Kate. Her brother even put some of the dirt in his toy Tonka truck and dumped it in. Everyone participated except for Aleta.

Her mind was made up. She was never, ever, going to say goodbye to Kate.

"Kate was the most intelligent dog I have ever known and always ready to please," said Aleta's dad. "She knew all the dog tricks like speak, sit, lie down, jump, roll over, shake hands, fetch, and stay. I could also tell her to leave the room or go outside and she'd do it. She had an uncanny knack for understanding what you wanted. Sometimes if I rushed to take her for a walk, she'd even poop and pee on command. Now that's a smart dog!"

This brought a smile to everyone's face, even Aleta's.

"Does anyone else want to share a favorite memory of Kate?" asked Aleta's dad.

"She was a great babysitter," her mom added. "I guess Collie's are naturals at that because they're herding dogs. They instinctively try to keep the flock together. When Aleta and her friends were toddlers and I needed them to stay in one place and play so I could keep an eye on them, Kate helped out. Any of the kids who tried to run or crawl away, Kate corralled them. She'd bark and race to block them so I could grab them and put them back with the other children. No one got too far away on her watch. Do you remember that, Aleta?"

Aleta nodded and grinned proudly.

"How about you girls? Ms. Moore, Ms. Fuentes…anything you'd like to share with us?" her dad asked, smiling at Cassie and Nina. Aleta could tell they were feeling shy as they shuffled their feet and exchanged looks.

Finally, Nina exclaimed, "Kate was soooo pretty with her long muzzle and tiny, sweet eyes. And when she walked on those dainty little paws, it was like watching a ballerina! I'll miss dressing her up and brushing her thick fur. She was the best looking model on four legs!"

"And the fastest!" Cassie quipped. "I loved playing chase with her and wrestling her, although she could wipe you out with that fluffy tail. And she was great at hide-and-go-seek. Aleta held her while we counted and looked for a place to hide. Then she'd let Kate go and she'd charge after us barking like crazy. If she found me, no matter how fast I ran, she always caught me!"

"Yeah, she could catch, too," Darnell chimed in. "I used to hit baseballs to her and she'd bring them back to me."

"Uh, uh, Darnell, not every time. Sometimes she'd keep the ball and make you chase after her," Aleta reminded him. "It was her dog joke."

"Oh, yeah," he said. "She would fake me out, too. A lot of times I fell down trying to get the ball from her. She was too quick! She'd have made a great running back in football!"

They all laughed, imagining Kate wearing football pads and a helmet. Aleta's mom leaned over and whispered in her ear, "This isn't so bad, huh?"

Aleta agreed. She really enjoyed hearing everyone talk about Kate. It made her feel a little better.

Uncle Jimmy cleared his throat a couple of times before speaking. "I don't think I can add much more to what you folks have already said about Kate. She was a beloved member of the Davis family. So I made a little present for y'all. I spent all night working on it. Aleta, would you do me the honors and open it?"

"Sure, Uncle Jimmy."

"Be careful. It's a little heavy."

He handed Aleta a package wrapped in newspapers. Everyone gathered around her as she removed the paper. She couldn't imagine what it might be. At first she thought it was just a block of polished mahogany wood.

Uncle Jimmy said, "Turn it over."

She turned it to the other side and was astounded to find a beautiful design that was hand carved and hand painted. The plaque had an image of a dog surrounded by a brightly colored wreath of flowers. At the top, the caption read:

IN MEMORY OF KATE
ONE OF THE WORLD'S GREATEST DOGS

They all gasped at the same time.

"This is absolutely gorgeous, Uncle Jimmy. Thank you so much," Aleta's mom said, her voice cracking.

"You're more than welcome, Melanie. I figure you folks can use this for a headstone or put it in the house somewhere."

"Thank you, Unc. I know we'll find a great place for it." Aleta's dad looked at Darnell and her. "Well, don't you kids have something to say to your uncle?"

Both were speechless. So, instead, they clamped their arms around Uncle Jimmy in a long and tight embrace.

"Now that's the kind of thank you I'm talking about," Uncle Jimmy remarked, hugging them back.

Aleta's dad rubbed his hands and looked around, "Does anyone else want to say a few words before we end? Aleta?"

There were lots of things Aleta wanted to say about Kate. "Kate was really friendly, but she could also be a great watch dog..."

"Yes, she was very protective," her dad agreed, nodding to everyone.

"...I never worried about anything because she slept at the foot of my bed. If she heard a strange noise at night, she'd jump up and run to the window and listen. She'd growl and bark, and then patrol the whole house. I always felt safe because I knew she was there. She even woke me up in the morning sometimes because she'd be lying next to me in the bed snoring."

Aleta laughed with everyone at first. But then it hit her again. Kate was dead. The sweetest, smartest, and most beautiful dog in the world was gone. And though she enjoyed sharing stories with everybody, Kate's death struck home again. Aleta's emotions flooded her like a tidal wave.

"I wish she were here now so I could pet her and hug her again."

Aleta felt her mom's hands rubbing her shoulders.

"No matter how I felt, no matter what I did, she was always there for me...but I wasn't there for her when she died."

"That's not your fault, darling," Aleta's mom said, stroking her hair.

"I really miss her, Mama...I want to see her...just one more time...I want her to come back! That's all...I want her back!"

The world felt like it was closing in on Aleta. She took off running.

"Aleta!" her mom yelled, but Aleta ignored her and kept sprinting. She needed to get away from all of this. And the only place she had to herself was her bedroom.

Aleta once heard that if you really wished for something badly enough it would come true. It may have sounded foolish, but she had to try. That night she got down on her knees and prayed beside the bed for Kate to return to her.

Aleta's mom overheard her.

"Aleta, do you mind if I come in?"

Aleta shrugged. Her mom sat beside her on the bed.

"Aleta, you know Kate's not coming back," her mom whispered tenderly.

"Yes she is!"

Aleta's mom cuddled her in her arms.

She cried, "Mama, it's not fair...how could she die? She wasn't that old."

"I know, darling," her mom sighed. "Sometimes life doesn't seem very fair to us. But even though Kate was only twelve, in dog years she was in her eighties. That means she was very old. She lived a long and happy life. You were a great friend to Kate and you treated her with kindness and respect. I've always been proud of you for that."

Aleta thought about what she said, but it didn't make her feel any better.

"Aleta, maybe one day we can get another dog..."

"No way! There's no dog like Kate." Aleta's head started aching. "Mama, can we stop talking about this?"

"Sure," her mom sighed and kissed her on the cheek. "Goodnight, sweetie. It doesn't seem like it right now, but give it time. Everything will turn out fine...you'll see."

Chapter 5

School's the Pits

Aleta truly wanted to believe her mom, but things got worse, not better. During P.E. class on Monday, they had to run laps around the field. Mr. Fellman jokingly hollered, "Come on, Aleta, you're moving slower than a tortoise. You can run faster than that!"

Aleta stopped running, planted her hands on her hips, and screamed, "You don't have to make fun of me! I'm just tired today, okay?!"

Mr. Fellman was so startled by her reaction that he dropped his clipboard. He didn't expect that from Aleta.

Ordinarily, Aleta had a great attitude and never minded joking around. Aleta figured Mr. Fellman planned to talk to her about what just happened, but once he saw the tears streaming down her cheeks, he let it go. He looked really concerned.

During science class, Mrs. Yoshida noticed her gazing out the window.

"Aleta, it might be a good idea to stop daydreaming and contribute to our discussion on biology. If you plan on being a veterinarian you need to—"

"I don't want to be one."

This stunned Mrs. Yoshida.

"What? But a month ago you wrote a report about how you wanted a career as a veterinarian because you loved animals so much."

"I changed my mind," Aleta replied coolly.

"Why?"

"Because what's the use of saving animals if they're going to die anyway?"

Mrs. Yoshida didn't have a chance to respond. Aleta burst into tears, right in the middle of class, and couldn't stop crying. She put her head down on her desk and wished she could disappear. Mrs. Yoshida escorted her out of the class and they sat down on one of the benches outside. The science instructor wasn't aware that Kate had died. Mrs. Yoshida told Aleta she was very sorry about the loss and said her door was always open if Aleta ever needed to talk.

It felt good to hear that from Mrs. Yoshida, but what Aleta really wanted was to leave. She asked to be excused so she could see the school nurse. School used to be her favorite place, but she didn't want to be there anymore.

Chapter 6

A Talk With Dad

The school nurse called Aleta's dad at his office and told him what had happened. Soon he was there to pick her up. In the car he said, "Tough day, huh?"

Aleta played with her fingers as she looked out her window.

"You want to talk about it? Aleta?"

"Daddy, can I go to a different school?"

"Going to another school is not going to change anything, honey."

"I don't want to go back."

"Why?"

"You won't understand," she said, still staring out the window.

"Why don't you give me a chance?"

She wrestled with her fingers some more and then finally said, "Because they probably think I'm a big crybaby. I cried in front of the whole class today! It was so embarrassing!"

"No it's not, Aleta. It's normal to cry when you're really sad. That's one of the ways we deal with grief."

"But in front of everyone? I'm sure they're all laughing at me."

"Honey, I don't think anyone is laughing at you. Before I picked you up, Mrs. Yoshida told me she explained to the class that you cried because your dog died. She said a lot of the students felt really bad for you. Some of them lost their pets at one time or another, too."

"Really?"

"That's right. We're not the only ones to lose a pet. Mrs. Yoshida said they had a big discussion about it in class."

They parked in front of their house but remained in the car.

"But Daddy, I'm scared. I feel like I want to cry a lot. I don't like to cry in front of the other kids."

"I know, sweetie. But it's natural to cry when someone you love dies. Don't fight it and don't be ashamed. There's nothing wrong with it. Grief can overcome you at the strangest and most surprising times. I know because it happened to me."

"To you?" Aleta was shocked.

"Oh yeah. Before you were born, my best friend, Phil Simons, died in a car accident. One night we were joking and laughing at a basketball game, the next day he was dead. And there was nothing I could do. I still think about Phil, and I still miss him."

Aleta looked at her dad. His eyes glistened with tears and he smiled, thinking of his old friend

"A week or so after his funeral, I was in a meeting at work and I suddenly started crying. I had to get out of there. At first I was embarrassed, but then I realized that I needed to cry. After that, I talked to some of my co-workers and they could relate to what I was going though because they had lost people they loved, too. I hadn't thought anybody understood what I was dealing with. But I was wrong. Sweetie, I want you to know you're not alone. People care about you. Your teachers, friends, and family. If you give us a chance, you'll see that we will always be there for you."

He kissed her tenderly on the forehead.

"Will you try it again and go to school tomorrow?"

"Okay, Daddy."

"Remember, don't sweat it if you cry."

"Okay." Aleta felt a little better, but she still felt kind of alone.

She grabbed her backpack and they got out of the car.

Chapter 7

Thinking of Kate

It was finally the annual weekend fair at Rose Park. But Aleta didn't go. She had a stomachache and wanted to stay home in bed. Aleta peeped through a slit in the curtains as she watched her mom and dad walk to the park with Darnell.

As soon as they were out of sight she went into the living room and slumped down on the couch. Aleta grabbed the remote control and clicked on the TV. She heard kids laughing and shoes slapping the pavement as they raced to the park. The picnic offered food, games, carnival rides, and lots of fun, but without Kate it just wouldn't be the same.

She jumped when the doorbell abruptly rang followed by urgent pounding on the door. Aleta instantly clicked off the TV and crept to the door. Before she could even look out the peephole she heard Cassie and Nina.

"Aleta! Aleeeeeeeetaaaa! Hey, are you home? Hello!" Cassie shouted.

She debated whether to answer.

"Cassie, I thought you said she was home?"

"That's what her mom told me. I thought I heard the TV."

"I don't hear anything. Hey, Aleta! You there?" An eye appeared in the peephole. Aleta ducked.

Aleta rubbed her forehead. She wished they would just go away. She really didn't want any company right now.

"I don't think she's there," Cassie sighed.

"Maybe she's asleep or something?"

"No. She would have heard us."

"Maybe she decided to go to the park after all." Nina sounded hopeful.

"Yeah, that's possible. Let's go check it out."

Aleta leaned against the door, relieved that they'd left. She felt bad because they were her closest friends, but she still thought that they couldn't truly understand what she was going through.

Sometimes she'd look around and feel like Kate was still in the house.

She went back to her room and gazed at the framed picture of Kate and her over her bed. In the photo her hands practically disappeared into Kate's mounds of fur. Both of them sported huge grins.

It seemed like Aleta thought about Kate now more than she ever did when Kate was alive. Whenever she heard barking, she looked around to see if it was Kate. It felt so empty in her room when she'd go to bed. Aleta would wake up and immediately stare at the foot of the bed. That was Kate's favorite place to sleep. Sometimes Aleta would let her sleep in the bed with her, even though her parents didn't like Kate on the bed because she often shed fur and it was hard to clean up. Every now and then Aleta still found tufts of fur that escaped being swept away in the corners of rooms or in the garage. Aleta knew it sounded silly, but she kept the fur she discovered in a plastic bag to remind her of Kate. Sometimes she'd look around and feel like Kate was still in the house. Aleta could feel Kate's presence. Almost like she was a ghost...

Chapter 8

Kate Returns!

That's when Aleta heard the loud flap of their dog door. Her heart started racing. Had her prayers been answered? Aleta's hair whipped across her face as she sped into the kitchen. The name unexpectedly flew out of her mouth: "Kate?"

Instead, she found her brother standing in the middle of the kitchen munching on chocolate chip cookies their mom baked earlier. He snatched another one from the platter.

"Lee, did I hear you say Kate?"

"Don't talk with food in your mouth!" she yelled. "Why didn't you use your key to come in?"

"It's more fun to come through the dog door."

"Well don't do that anymore!"

"What are you so mad about?"

Aleta shook her forefinger at him. "Darnell, you've got crumbs all over the floor! Mama's gonna get mad!"

"I was gonna clean it up!"

"Just get out of here! I'll do it." Aleta shook her head as she grabbed the sponge.

"Thanks!" he yelled happily, plucking another cookie and spilling more crumbs on the floor before running out of the kitchen. He scrambled through the closet and pulled out his baseball bat and glove.

After she finished cleaning up, Aleta fumed as she marched into her bedroom and slammed the door. *Darnell is so messy,* she thought. But what really irritated her was that he seemed happy. Unlike her, he was running around and having fun again. Was she the only one in this family that really cared about Kate being gone?

There was a soft knock at her bedroom door.

"Can I come in?"

"No!"

"Lee, you ought to come to the park. Man, they got all kind of rides there. They got this big old ride that whips you around and around…it's so cool!"

She rolled her eyes. "That's great, Darnell."

"I saw Cassie and Nina at the park."

"Wonderful."

"They asked me if I knew where you were."

"What did you say?"

"I said you were at home."

"Thanks a lot."

"What are you doing?"

"None of your…"

And that's when Aleta decided to teach Darnell a lesson about using Kate's dog door. She was mad from cleaning up behind him, but she was also sick of Darnell acting so happy. Why should he be so happy when Kate's dead?

"I'm playing with Kate."

Silence. And then she heard a very weak, "What did you say?"

She opened up the door grinning from ear to ear. Darnell stood frozen at the doorway, holding his bat and glove. Aleta skipped past him and whistled. He didn't know what to think as he followed her into the living room.

Suddenly, Aleta turned and said, "Sit! Good girl!"

Darnell eyed her suspiciously. "What's wrong with you?"

"So, what do you think?"

"About what?"

"You know what."

Silence.

"Come on, Darnell…about Kate being back!"

His eyes got big and he said, "That's not funny, Lee."

"I'm serious, Darnell. Don't you hear her barking?"

"No." Squinting, Darnell looked around him. "How come I can't see her?"

"Because she's a ghost, silly. Look! Now she's jumping on you."

Darnell warily stepped back.

"You're being mean, Lee. I'm gonna tell Mama!"

"Darnell, it's the truth. Kate really is alive! She's a ghost!"

Darnell dropped his bat and glove. He was three blinks from crying.

Sniffling, he said, "Stop teasing me, Aleta. You're just making fun of me 'cause you know I'm afraid to turn the lights off at night!"

At that moment, their dad walked in.

Chapter 9

Time for Help

"Hey, kids, what's happening?" their dad said, snapping and doing a silly walk.

"Aleta told me that Kate—" She clapped a hand over Darnell's mouth.

"Okay…what kind of secret do you kids have this time?" He grabbed a newspaper and plopped down in his lounge chair.

"Who ate all the cookies?" their mom asked from the kitchen.

"Aleta—" she managed to cover her brother's mouth again.

Their mom walked into the living room.

"Aleta? I'm glad your appetite's back but it's going to make you sick."

"I didn't eat any cookies."

"Well, then, who did?"

The room was quiet.

Darnell snatched Aleta's hand from his mouth, "Lee said Kate is a ghost!"

Their dad peered up from his newspaper. "What did you just say?"

Aleta bowed her head and covered her face. She wished she were an only child.

"She said Kate's a ghost and she's in our house! Is that true, Mama?"

Their mom and dad exchanged worried glances.

"Aleta, did you tell your brother that? Well, did you?"

"Yes, Daddy."

"Do you really believe that? Huh?"

Aleta slowly shook her head.

"Yeah, I see her now, too, Lee." Darnell pointed towards the fireplace.

"Sweetheart, I think we need to talk," said Aleta's mom. "Sit down with me on the couch."

Aleta's mom placed an arm around her shoulders. "Honey, you know better than to tell stories. Doing that to your little brother is just plain cruel…"

Aleta nodded.

"…And sometimes it causes more harm than good."

"Why did you do that?" her dad wanted to know.

"I don't know…I guess I was just angry at him."

"There are other ways to handle your anger."

"I know, Daddy. I'm sorry," Aleta mumbled.

Meanwhile, her embarrassing brother tiptoed around the room cooing, "Kate. Come here, Kate." As usual, he was making things worse.

"Darnell, will you cool it?!" their dad demanded. "Kate is not a ghost and there are no ghosts in this house. Don't let me have to tell you again." He sat rigidly in his chair, brows furrowed with concern and toying with his mustache.

"Yes, sir." Darnell looked disappointed.

"And, by the way, your sister has something to tell you," their dad said as he shot Aleta a look.

"I'm sorry I lied to you, Darnell."

"That's okay, Lee. Hey, Mama, are there any more cookies?"

"No. Aren't you on your way to the park? We need to talk to your sister."

"Oh, okay. Bye." Darnell grabbed his bat and glove. Surprisingly, he looked at Aleta sympathetically rather than with his usual glee of seeing her in trouble.

"Bye, Lee," he said before shutting the door.

Aleta stood nervously in front of her parents, eyes glued to the floor.

"Aleta, I want you to go to your room until you learn how to behave properly," her dad said. "Believe me, we know how close you and Kate were and how much you miss her. We all do. But pretending Kate is a ghost is going too far. It's ridiculous! And it just makes things harder for everyone. Sometimes when we really love someone, it's difficult for us to accept it when they're no longer there. But sooner or later we have to move forward." Then he looked sad. Aleta finally saw that he missed Kate a lot, too.

"Yes, Daddy."

"Wait. Don't leave yet, Aleta." Her mom patted her dad's arm. "Ben, I have another idea."

"Okay, let's hear it," her dad said sitting back in his chair.

"Your dad's right, we ought to send you to your room. But what you need more than anything, Aleta, is some fresh air and to be around your friends again. You might even want to say hi to Uncle Jimmy. You agree, Ben?"

"Absolutely. I'm sure Uncle Jimmy would love to see you," he said.

"So, why don't you go outside, go to the park, and play with your friends."

"But I don't really want to, I—"

"You don't have a choice, young lady."

"Yes, Ma'am."

Chapter 10

Visiting Uncle Jimmy

Aleta trudged out the door and headed to Rose Park. Wandering through the park, Aleta took her parents' advice and went to find Uncle Jimmy.

"Well, I declare, if it ain't the prettiest girl this side of the Mississippi!"

"Hi, Uncle Jimmy."

He stood in the rose garden wearing a gray work shirt and pants and tending his beautiful flowers.

"Guess what, young lady? I knew you were coming here," he said, eyes dancing. "These flowers get jealous whenever

38

you're around because you're prettier than they are. That's why they are standing straight and tall. Before you showed up, I couldn't get them to act right to save my soul!" He threw his head back and howled with laughter.

"Thank you, Uncle Jimmy."

It was hard not to smile as she gazed into his dark face whose beard was crusted with silver hairs. He lovingly caressed his prize flowers.

"So tell me, honey, why you got the blues in those brown eyes of yours? You should be out there having fun with the rest of the kids."

Aleta studied the ground, not sure what to say.

He knelt down, placed his scissors in the soil, and lightly tapped her on the forehead. "What's on your mind? Don't take no brain surgeon to know something's wrong."

Gazing into those kind eyes, Aleta realized there was nothing to fear.

"Uncle Jimmy…do you believe in ghosts?"

"Ghosts? Girl, where do you come up with questions like that?"

He pulled a couple of weeds from around the plants. "Ghosts, huh? This old boy's been around for quite a while, seen a lot of things, but I can't ever say I've seen a ghost. Course, I've never met anyone who could prove they don't exist, either. Why you asking?"

"I got in trouble for telling Darnell that Kate is a ghost."

"Hmmmm…I see. So do you believe she's a ghost?"

"Kinda…sometimes I feel like she's still around, watching me. But I know she isn't really there."

"I felt the same way when my dog died," he mused, sliding off his cap and scratching his head.

"You mean, you don't think I'm crazy?" Aleta gasped.

"You? Crazy? Naaaah."

He shielded his eyes from the sun.

"Let me tell you about crazy. When I was your age, I had a dog named Patches. Called him that because he had as many spots on his body as I have white hairs on my head. Patches was up there in age. One day while I was playing in a field, someone called out my name. Honey, I looked around and didn't see anybody. That's strange because my eyes are as sharp  as a hunting knife. Finally, I looked into some bushes and found Patches lying on his side, limp as a wet towel. Poor old Patches. His soul had gone to the great beyond. But I wonder to this day if it wasn't Patches that shouted out my name before he died."

"Really, Uncle Jimmy?"

"Sure, girl. Now you try telling people about a talking dog. The kids laughed at me from schoolyard to schoolyard, but I didn't care because in my heart I believed Patches said goodbye to me. We were tighter than words to a book. And maybe Patches never really did talk. Seems possible I needed to believe he did to help me get through my grief over his death."

Clasping his hand, she said to him, "I believe you, Uncle Jimmy."

"Thank you, child. I appreciate that," he replied, gently squeezing Aleta's hand.

They sat quietly thinking their own thoughts and enjoying the sweet smell of roses and the warm caress of the sun. After a few minutes, Uncle Jimmy turned to her and said in a voice as soothing as warm lemon and honey, "You see, Aleta, no one lives forever. That's what makes us so special. We are only here for a short while so we have to make the best of it. That's the way life is. You never know what the next day will bring."

Aleta wrapped her arms around her knees as she slowly rocked back and forth. It made her sad again to think about Kate, but she knew deep down inside Uncle Jimmy was right. Tears eased their way into her eyes as she stared at the ground.

He gently cupped her face in his warm hands, as if she were one of his roses, and offered something she'd never forget. "Aleta, in a sense, you are right. Kate is here with you. And even if you can't see her, she'll always be there. She'll always be a part of your life, even in death."

He became really quiet, but then a big smile leapt across his face.

"I do believe some folks are trying to get your attention."

Aleta looked up to see Cassie and Nina waving in the distance.

She waved back.

"Looks to me like they really miss you."

Now they were making funny faces, doing jumping jacks, and beckoning for her to join them.

Uncle Jimmy kissed her on the cheek. "Go on, girl.

Sometimes the best remedy in the world is to be with your friends when you're feeling down."

She ambled towards Cassie and Nina. They ran and met her halfway. They stood facing each other.

"What's up, doc?"

"Nothing. What's up with you, Cassie?"

"The sky, the sun, the moon…"

"Okay, okay, I get it."

"We miss you," Nina remarked, stroking her arm. "Do you want to talk? We can talk if you want to."

"Thanks, but I just want to hang out."

"Do you want to take a ride on the roller coaster?" Cassie's eyes twinkled.

"That sounds like fun."

"Now you're talking." Cassie locked arms with Aleta on one side and Nina on the other. They whisked her away to the Rose Park "Thorn In Your Side" roller coaster ride. It was hard for Aleta to think about her problems when she was speeding downhill on a roller coaster and screaming at the top of her lungs.

Chapter 11

Remembering Kate

When Aleta stepped into the house her parents were seated on the couch, anxious expressions on their faces. Her dad immediately put down his magazine. "Hey, baby girl."

"Hi."

"Whoa!" her dad said. "Is it my imagination or do I see a smile on your face?"

"Yeah, I guess." She grinned self-consciously as she played with her hair.

Her mom asked, "Did you have a good time at the park?"

"Yes."

Her dad sat up in his chair. "You see Cassie and Nina?"

"Uh, huh. We hung out and went on some rides. It was fun."

"That's great," her mom remarked. "I bet they were happy to see you."

"Uh, huh."

Her dad said, "Oh, Uncle Jimmy called. Told us you guys had a nice talk."

"Uh, huh."

"Well it looks like you've had quite a day, Aleta," her mom exclaimed. "You feeling better?" she asked, studying her face.

Aleta crossed her arms and swayed nervously from side to side. "Yes, but, um, Mama? Daddy? I'm…"

"Yeah? Go ahead, kid, we're listening," her dad said gently.

"I'm sorry about how I've been acting."

Aleta's mom reached out. "Come here, baby…you don't have to apologize. Kate's death has been rough on all of us."

She jumped on the couch and snuggled between them. Her mom started redoing her hair.

"Just so you know," her dad said, "You're not alone. We miss Kate as much as you do. That dog was one of the family. I'm so glad Uncle Jimmy made us that plaque. We can look at it and always remember Kate. She is a memory worth cherishing."

"Would it be okay if I put the plaque in my room?"

Her dad looked at her mom and they both nodded. He said, "Sounds like a winner."

Aleta squeezed both of their arms and held them tightly.

Her mom snapped her fingers excitedly. "Speaking of memories, I've got an idea. Why don't we start a family project this week? We can scour the house for every picture we have of Kate and put together a scrapbook dedicated to her? We'll just keep adding to it as we find things."

"Melanie, I think you've got something there," her dad agreed. "And Aleta, we can take our time to do this. It might be a little tough to look at pictures of Kate sometimes, so just let us know if this gets too hard. Hey, do you still have all those drawings and illustrations you did of Kate when you were little? They can go into a scrapbook, too."

"They can?"

"Sure."

"I've got hundreds of those! I kept them in a box under my bed. And Cassie told me she still had photos from some of those doggy fashion shoots we used to do of Kate."

Now Aleta got excited about the project, too.

"Well what are we waiting on, people? Let's get started," her mom said dancing around the room and pulling open drawers.

"I'm going to my room right now!" Aleta dashed to her bedroom.

"Grab your brother while you're at it. He's in his room playing video games."

"Okay, Daddy," she yelled back.

Kate is a memory worth cherishing.

Later that evening Aleta wore a huge smile on her face as she sat on the bed with the plaque in her lap. It was so smooth and shiny. She liked the way it felt. There was a noise behind her and she glanced back to see her brother standing forlornly at her doorway.

"You want to come in?" she asked.

"Sure!" Darnell replied, shocked to be invited in as he jumped onto Aleta's bed and sat happily beside her.

"Can I see the plaque, too?"

"Sure."

Now they were both holding it admiringly.

"Kate's not really a ghost, is she, Lee?"

"No. I'm sorry for teasing you. I was just mad that day and really wanted her to be with us again."

"That's all right. I understand."

They were quiet for a while until Darnell looked up at her with melancholy eyes.

"Aleta, I really miss Kate."

"Yeah, me, too."

Aleta surprised herself by putting her arm around Darnell. He snuggled into her.

"Wanna get another dog someday, Lee?"

"Maybe...someday...I don't think I'm ready right now."

"Naaah, me either. Hey, Lee...I mean, you don't have to...but, you wanna play some cards?"

"Sure!"

"What? You do? Really? Okay...don't go anywhere. I'll be right back."

He leaped off the bed and charged into the closet to get his cards. Aleta couldn't help but laugh at his excitement. Little brothers weren't so bad after all.

In the days and weeks that followed, Aleta played and laughed a lot more with her family and friends. And the

Davises put together a beautiful scrapbook that they left on the coffee table for everyone to view.

She thought, *I guess Uncle Jimmy was right. That is the way life is. You never know what the next day will bring.*

Coping With Your Pet's Death

Even though you know that animals (and people) don't live forever, when your dog or cat, hamster or goldfish dies, you can feel so sad. It just doesn't seem fair! You may not know what to do or what to say. You might feel afraid or embarrassed to cry in front of other kids or your parents or siblings. Maybe you want to be alone because you feel like no one can understand what you're feeling and think that nothing can make you feel better. It's okay to feel sad and lonely and angry when your pet dies. It's perfectly normal! You've lost a big part of your life, "someone" very special to you, and it is sad. But no matter how you are feeling right now, know that someday you'll feel better and you'll be able to remember your pet with happiness. Here are a few things you can do to get through the tough times right after your pet dies:

Talk about it. You can talk to your parents, other relatives or trusted adults, or your school counselor about how you're feeling. When you do, you can ask them questions about your pet's death or death itself if you like and if you think that will help you feel better. You can talk to your friends, too. They might understand what you're going through, or they can be there to just listen, too.

Get your feelings out. Don't hold your feelings inside. It's okay to be sad and miss your pet. If you don't feel like talking, you can always express your feelings in other ways, like crying, doing artwork, or writing or journaling (which you don't have to show others). You could even dance out your feelings, just as long as you get them out.

Coach yourself. Talk yourself through your sadness, anger, and any other feelings. Check in with yourself about how you're feeling and remind yourself that you can get through it. Kind of like a "feelings pep talk." You might say, "I'm feeling sad now, but I can talk to Mom about this and I'll feel better later" or "I feel so angry about Kate's death, but I can try to paint my feelings and maybe that will help."

Memorialize your pet. You can keep your pet's memory alive in a lot of ways. You can put out photos of your pet and you (or the whole family) together. You can make a scrapbook or a photo album with your favorite pictures and mementos. You can even plant a tree or garden in your pet's memory or write a poem or story about your pet. Talk to your family and friends about having a memorial service for your pet so that you can say "goodbye." Your family and friends might have some other ideas for this, too, so go ahead and ask them.

The death of a pet is sad and difficult. Feeling lots of strong emotions now is normal. But you don't have to go through it alone. Remember that you can and will get through this with the help of your family and friends.